BUS RIDE

by Marilyn Sachs

with drawings by Amy Rowen

A SKINNY BOOK

E. P. DUTTON NEW YORK

Library of Congress Cataloging in Publication Data

Sachs, Marilyn. Bus ride.
(A Skinny book)

SUMMARY: Two high school juniors who consider themselves losers get to know each other while riding the bus to school.
I. Rowen, Amy. II. Title.
PZ7.S1187Bu [Fic] 79–23596
ISBNs: 0–525–27325–5 [hardcover] 0–525–45048–3 [paperback]

Published in the United States by E. P. Dutton, a Division of Elsevier-Dutton Publishing Company, Inc., New York

Published simultaneously in Canada by Clarke, Irwin & Company Limited, Toronto and Vancouver

Editor: Ann Durell Designer: Stacie Rogoff

Printed in the U.S.A.
10 9 8 7 6 5 4 3 2

For Laurel and Mark Benjamin

· 1 ·

MONDAY

"Ouch!"

"Excuse me."

"It's all right."

"Didn't I step on your foot?"

"It's okay."

"I never saw the bus this crowded before. I think there were a couple that didn't run at all. I was waiting at least twenty-five minutes."

"Me too. I'm late for my first-period class."

"What class is it?"

"Biology."

"Who's your teacher?"

"Mr. Shaw."

"I had a lot of trouble with him last year. He's a real nerd."

"I know. He probably won't believe the bus was late. He never believes any of the kids. I hate him."

"Mr. Hori is okay. You should have taken him for biology."

"I wanted to but he wasn't teaching this term."

"How come?"

"I think he had some kind of a breakdown. My girl friend said she heard he was in a hospital."

"Who's your girl friend?"

"Oh, I guess it was Linda Breslin. Why?"

"I thought maybe I knew her."

"Linda Breslin?"

"No, somebody else."

"Who?"

"Well—Karen Shepherd. She's a friend of yours too, isn't she?"

"Karen Shepherd?"

She looked up into the boy's face, very, very close to her own on the crowded bus. He looked familiar but she couldn't place him. What was he? He was too tall for a sophomore. Probably a junior like her. But she didn't think he had ever been in any of her classes. Maybe she'd seen him in the halls or the lunchroom or maybe just on the bus.

He was looking intently at her now. She moved her head slightly so he wouldn't see all the pimples on the left side of her face. Today the right side was clear. Last week it had been the left side. Never were both sides clear at the same time.

"Yes, she's your friend, isn't she?"

"Sort of—but how did you know?"

"I saw you together a few times. Once you were eating lunch with her. Another time you were walking down the hall together. And then I saw you both on the bus last Wednesday."

"Last Wednesday?"

"Yes. I never saw her on the bus before. I thought she lived over on Fulton."

"She does, but I guess she was coming from her father's house last week. Her parents are divorced, and every once in a while she sleeps over at his house during the week."

"Oh—that's why. I never saw her on the bus before."

"No, she usually doesn't ride this bus."

"I was surprised to see her. I thought maybe she might be moving or something."

"No, she's not moving."

"I know you take the bus because I see you every day."

"Yes, I take the bus."

They nodded at each other, and then there didn't seem to be anything further to say. More and more people pushed onto the bus, and when it was time to get off, he was way ahead of her. She could see him hurrying along the street towards school as she stepped off at the rear exit.

· 2 ·

TUESDAY

"Did Mr. Shaw give you a hard time?"

"Oh! Hi! No. That kid near the door, Jim Moore, is in my class. So because two of us told him the bus was late, he had to believe us. He didn't want to. He hates kids."

The boy laughed. He had crooked front teeth and a kind of high, baying laugh. But his skin was smooth and clear, damn it. Today there was a whole new clump of pimples on her forehead. She had to comb her hair down low and sideways on the left side to hide them.

He had a sharp, prominent Adam's apple. It wobbled up and down as he prepared to speak.

"You're a junior, aren't you?"

"Yes—are you?"

"Uh-huh. I saw you at the assembly last week for class officers. Who'd you vote for?"

"Let me see— Oh—I voted for Rita Apple for president. What about you?"

"I voted for Bruce Harris. Who else did you vote for?"

"I have to think. None of them got in. Oh yes—I voted for Al Rogers for vice-president, and Rosie Yamamoto for secretary, and Ellen Lee for treasurer."

"Why'd you vote for Rosie Yamamoto?"

"Why? Well, because I like her. She's on the speech team with me, and she's a smart girl and a nice girl. Do you know her?"

"Yes. She's in my film lit class. She's okay, but I figured you'd vote for Karen."

"Karen?"

"Sure. Karen Shepherd. She ran for secretary and she got in by a lot of votes. How come you didn't vote for her? She's your friend, isn't she?"

"She's sort of my friend."

"And she's real smart too, and everybody likes her."

He was looking earnestly at her. His eyebrows seemed to ripple towards each other. It irritated her the way his eyebrows moved.

"I guess so," she said carefully.

"So how come you didn't vote for her?"

"Because it's a free country," she told him, and pushed her way further into the back of the bus.

· 3 ·

WEDNESDAY

"What's your name, anyway?"

"Judy Koppelmacker."

"What?"

"Judy Koppelmacker. What's so funny?"

"Nothing. Nothing. I'm Ernie Russe."

"Nothing so great about your name either."

"Okay, don't get excited."

Judy kept her eyes on his face, just waiting for him to laugh again.

"It's a perfectly good German name," she told him coldly.

"That's nice."

"No, it's not nice. You don't know what it is to be stuck with a crummy name like Koppelmacker. Every time a teacher calls the roll,

some birdbrain is sure to laugh out loud. I'm going to change it legally when I'm eighteen. I don't care what my father says. I hate it."

"What are you going to change it to?"

"Jones."

"Jones? That's no name."

"Sure it's a name. Judy Jones. I like the way it sounds."

"It sounds ordinary."

"Too bad. If you were stuck with a name like Koppelmacker for sixteen years, you'd be glad to sound ordinary too."

"To tell you the truth, I think it's a shame not to keep a name the way it is. The way it was, I mean. It sort of gives you roots. Everybody's looking for roots nowadays. Doesn't it make you feel good to think that you come from a long line of Koppelmackers?"

"Are you being funny?"

"No—honestly. If you change your name to Jones, you'll lose your place, sort of. All those Koppelmackers will come to a dead end because of you."

"That's fine with me."

"You know, it's funny because my name was shortened. When my great grandfather came over from Italy, he wanted a more American-sounding name. So he shortened it from Russolini to Russe."

"He was one smart man, I think. Russe is a lot nicer than Russolini. It sounds like Mussolini."

"So what if it does?"

"Well, I wouldn't want a name that sounds like Mussolini."

"So what do you think Jones sounds like? Bones . . . groans . . . moans . . ."

"You're just being stupid."

"No, I'm not. I think I'll change my name back to Russolini when I'm eighteen. I'm proud of my heritage. Why do I have to sound blah and ordinary? Thanks for helping me make up my mind."

"Don't mention it."

· 4 ·

THURSDAY

"You still mad?"

"I wasn't mad."

"Sure you were. You stuck your nose in a book and wouldn't look at me."

"I was studying. It had nothing to do with you. Shaw gave us an exam yesterday. So that's why I had my nose in the book."

"How'd you do?"

"Terribly. I probably failed."

"Probably the best thing is not to study at all. With a teacher like that, nothing helps. Next time try doing nothing and see what happens."

"You're right." Judy grinned at him. "It can't be any worse. That's for sure."

He didn't look Italian because he had pale blue

eyes and sort of sandy-colored blond hair. A funny-looking boy—but funny-looking in a nice way. There were kids she knew at school who were nice-looking in a funny way. Like Jamie Lucas who looked like a rock star. But his eyes blinked all the time and he spit when he talked. Or Melanie Winters, a really beautiful blonde girl with a fantastic suntan. But she had a way of scrunching up her face and laughing too loud. She had bad breath too.

But this boy—Ernie Russe—had eyes that were too small, a mouth that was too big, but a kind of sparkle about his face. He looked—funny but nice. She really wasn't mad at him.

"I really wasn't mad at you," she told him again.

"That's good because I wanted to ask you something."

"Me?"

"Yeah—but I don't know. Hey—look—over there—both of them are getting up. Hurry!"

"Excuse me— Oh, I'm sorry—excuse me."

"Here, go on, sit down."

Politely he stood beside the empty seats and let her slide in first. Thank goodness, they were on the left side of the bus so her pimples were facing away from him. It was exciting having a boy stand to one side, and just a little tantalizing to brush against him as you slid by.

"How's that for luck?"

"Fantastic!"

They smiled at each other. There were laugh lines around his eyes, and a faint furry fuzz over his lip and under his soft, smooth chin.

"Judy?"

"Yes?"

"Look, can I tell you something?"

"Sure you can, Ernie."

"It's about Karen."

"Oh."

"I guess you probably figured me out already—the way I kept asking you all those questions about her."

"That's right. You did."

"I guess you got angry because I kept asking questions about her, and you really didn't know me or anything about me."

"Well . . ."

"Nobody likes to tell stories about their friends."

"She's sort of a friend."

"Unless they know why."

"Ernie—what is it?"

"Wait—just let me tell you a little more. Then

you'll understand. See—believe it or not—I'm really a very shy person."

"No, you're not."

"Well, with you I'm not, but—well—when there's somebody I really like—I mean, like Karen Shepherd—I don't know what to say or do. She was in my bio class last year when I just transferred to Washington. I never saw a girl like her before. She's so pretty—sort of like a big blonde cat . . . with those wonderful green eyes. I never saw eyes like that before. Did you?"

"Mmm."

"But it isn't because she's so pretty. It's everything else—the way she laughs, and how nice she is to everybody. Every time she sees me, she gives me such a big smile, and . . ."

"She does that with everybody."

"Yes, I know. Everybody likes her—she's such a . . . such a nice girl. And one day when I was absent, she got the homework assignment for me. I didn't ask her to do it. She just came over to my desk the next day and smiled at me, and said, 'Here, Ernie, I got the assignment for you.' She's such a . . . such a . . ."

"Nice girl?"

"Yeah, a real nice girl."

"Well, Ernie, I don't think . . ."

"Wait, I know what you're going to say, but let me finish. I'm going to feel real stupid after this is over, so I may as well tell you everything. She's very popular. I know that. She's got a million guys after her, but somebody told me that she just broke up with Ted Cooper. She was going around with him all of last term, and lately I never see them together. Is it true?"

"Yes, she broke up with Ted Cooper."

"Why did she?"

"I think he broke up with her."

"I don't believe it."

"Well, go ask him."

"I don't know him. But why do you say he broke up with her?"

"Because she told me."

"Karen told you?"

"Yes."

"She told you he broke up with her?"

"Yes."

"But why? Why would he break up with her? Why would anybody break up with Karen Shepherd?"

"Look, I don't really think . . ."

"No, I don't mean to pry. All I really want to know for sure is that she's not going around with Ted Cooper anymore."

"No, she's not."

"Because maybe if she's not, I can ask her to go out with me. I know she likes me. She always says, 'Hi, Ernie,' or 'What's doing, Ernie?' or 'How are you, Ernie?' And when school let out for the Christmas holidays, she said, 'So long, Ernie. Have fun.' I should have said to her, 'I'll have more fun if you have it with me.' I think of lots of things I could have said to her when she talks to me. But I always think of them too late—after it's happened. Anyway, now that she's not going around with Ted Cooper, I have a couple of ideas. I thought I'd ask you what you thought."

"But why me?"

"Because you're her friend, and you know her."

"I'm sort of her friend."

"You can tell me the kinds of things she likes to do— I mean, I can do all sorts of things. If she likes movies—we could go to the movies—or maybe she likes music. We could go to a concert. I don't care what kind of music—I'll even go to a punk-rock concert if she likes. Maybe she'd rather play miniature golf or go bowling. Now that she's free . . ."

"She's not free."

"But didn't you say she broke up with Ted Cooper?"

KAREN

"Yes, I did."

"And she's not going around with anybody else. I see her in school. She's always with a different group of kids."

"She's going out with a guy who goes to—to City College. She's not free."

· 5 ·

FRIDAY

"What's his name?"

"Whose name?"

"The guy Karen Shepherd is going out with."

"Oh him! Uh . . . Alan, I think."

"Alan who?"

"I'm not sure."

"Is it Alan Hall, Mindy Hall's brother?"

"No, I don't think so. What difference does it make?"

"I just would like to know. What's he like?"

"Oh—let me see—what did she tell me? Oh yeah—he's tall, dark, and handsome, and very smart."

"If he's so smart, why's he going to City?"

"I guess his family can't afford to send him anyplace else. But he's very smart."

"How old is he?"

"What did she say—nineteen, I think."

"That's too old for her."

"She likes them old."

"That's just great."

Judy looked with satisfaction at the sorrowing lines around his mouth and eyes. Evidently he had it bad for Karen, but he'd get over it. This was a good time to change the subject.

"What are you taking this term?"

"Nothing great—civics, auto repair, French, film lit, American history, and P.E."

"Film lit's pretty much Mickey Mouse, isn't it?"

He shrugged impatiently. She could see he was thinking about something else, so she said, "I'm taking biology, creative writing, German, typing, trig, and tennis."

"Mmm."

"The only decent teacher I have is Mrs. Barnes, for creative writing. She's great."

"Mmm."

"She's young and wears jeans and she lets you call her Sandy if you like."

"Mmm."

"My typing teacher, Ms. Henderson, is a real shlug. I hate her. So does Karen."

"Who?"

"Karen. Karen Shepherd."

"Is she in your typing class?"

"Yes, she is."

"What period is it?"

"The fourth."

"And what room is it?"

"116."

"Look, do you think . . . Oh, forget it."

"Forget what?"

"Well, I was thinking . . . it's right before lunch, so I was wondering—maybe I could come by and say hi to you—and Karen—and maybe—Where does she have lunch anyway?"

"Usually with the kids in drama. In room 208."

"What about you?"

"Well, I usually bring along a sandwich and eat it outside, near the girls' gym."

"No, I mean do you ever have lunch with Karen?"

"Once in a while. Not usually."

"Well, could you . . . would you . . ."

"Ernie, she's got a boyfriend."

"I know, but maybe . . ."

"Besides, I'm busy today."

"How about Monday?"

"I'm busy Monday too."

"Why are you so angry?"

"I'm not angry but I think I'm going to study now."

"Study what? You're looking in your typing book. You can't study typing."

"I can if I want to. Why don't you just leave me alone?"

"Listen, Judy Koppelmacker . . ."

"Stop it!"

"Stop what?"

"Stop calling me Judy Koppelmacker."

"Okay, okay, listen Judy! Listen Judy Jones! How's that? Good, good! Now you're smiling."

"What do you want?"

"Look, you do me a favor, and I'll do you one."

"I don't need a favor."

"Maybe you will one day."

"Okay, what do you want?"

"How about asking Karen to have lunch with you and me? You can say I'm a friend of yours. . . . No, wait! Maybe you better not say that."

"Why not?"

"Well . . ."

"You mean because then she might not think much of your taste if she thought the two of us were friends."

"No, no, but . . ."

"And you don't want to have any friends you're ashamed of. Well listen, neither do I!"

"Take it easy, Judy. You blow up over nothing. Where are you going? Wait up!"

· 6 ·

MONDAY

"Have a nice weekend?"

"Mmm."

"What are you reading today?"

"Don't bother me."

"That's a funny name for a book."

"Go away."

"You know, you have a nice smile. You should try using it more often."

"Look, Russe, I'm not interested. . . ."

"And you've really got a pretty mouth when it's not all tightened up. You've got pretty hair too, except you wear it in such a funny way. Look how lopsided it is on this side. Why don't you push it back like . . ."

"Stop it! Leave my hair alone!"

"Okay, okay. I just thought— Why do you wear it that way anyway? It looks funny."

"Why don't you just mind your own business."

"Because I'd like to be friends with you."

"Only because you want something out of me."

"Well, maybe that's what friendship is all about."

"You mean using people for your own selfish purposes?"

"No, I mean getting things from them and giving things back. I still don't know why you're sore, but most friendships are based on give and take."

"But with you it's all take. You're only interested in me because you think you can get to Karen through me. You think I can help you."

"So what's so terrible about that?"

"Nothing, except you're talking about friendship, and that's just bull. You don't want to be friends with me, so why pretend?"

"Sure I do. I just said I did."

"Why?"

"Because we've got things in common."

"Like what?"

"Well—we ride the bus together."

"Big deal!"

"And we both hate Mr. Shaw. . . ."

"You should have lots of friends in school over that one."

"And . . . well . . . never mind."

"Go on! What else?"

"You won't like it."

"I don't like any of this so you may as well be honest for a change."

"Okay, Judy Koppelmacker—I mean Jones—I will tell you. I figure we're both alike in another way too."

"Go ahead."

"I have no luck with girls, and I guess—I mean I think—well . . ."

"You think I have no luck with boys, right?"

"You made me say it."

"Okay. Well, you're mistaken. I have all the luck I want."

"Fine! Okay! I apologize. All right?"

"Lots of guys have been interested in me."

"Mmm."

"There was George Reilly in eighth grade. He was very interested in me."

"How'd you know?"

"I just knew."

"Okay, let's just forget it."

"And last term, this guy, Henry Wilner, he really liked me."

"Yeah?"

"You don't believe me?"

"Sure, I do."

"No, you don't."

"Well, who have you ever liked who liked you back?"

"None of your business."

"Fine. Why don't we change the subject?"

"No, I don't want to. Why did you say I don't have any luck with boys? Why do you think I don't?"

"It's a feeling I have about you."

"But I want to know why."

"Well, you're so tense, and kind of jumpy. You're not bad-looking, and if you wore your hair . . ."

"Forget about my hair!"

"But Judy, what I was thinking was—we could be friends. It's true, at first I only wanted to get to know you because you were Karen's friend. . . ."

"See!"

"Wait! But now I was thinking, we could really help each other. I mean you help me with Karen . . ."

"She has a boyfriend."

"But he goes to City, and she doesn't see him every day. Anyway, you help me and I'll help you."

"How?"

"There must be some boy you like, and maybe I could help you get together with him."

"I don't need your help."

"Think it over, Judy."

· 7 ·

TUESDAY

"I thought it over."

"And?"

"I accept."

"Great! I was afraid you were never going to speak to me again."

"Well, I was pretty sore at first, because it hurts to have somebody else find out what you've been hiding for years and years."

"What do you mean?"

"That I'm a loser."

"I didn't say that, Judy."

"No, but you thought it."

"No, I didn't. I just . . ."

"It's all right. It's true. I am a loser and I never really admitted it to myself until yesterday."

"Hey, you're crying. Look, Judy, I really don't think you're a loser. Don't cry!"

"Shh! Everybody'll hear."

"They can't help hearing. We're packed so tight together. Do you need a sleeve?"

"No, it's okay. If you can just hand me the tissue in my jacket pocket. I can't get my elbow down."

"Here it is."

"Thanks. Anyway, I didn't tell you the truth yesterday."

"It doesn't matter."

"It does to me. George Reilly, that boy I told you about in the eighth grade, wasn't interested in me. I was interested in him. He was interested in dogs. He had a picture of a Doberman in his wallet."

"He sounds like a real turkey."

"No, he was a very nice boy. Last term, Henry Wilner, you know, I told you he liked me."

"Yeah?"

"Well, he didn't—and he's not a nice boy the way George Reilly was. He's a little, skinny guy with freckles. . . ."

"He can't help that."

"Shut up a minute and let me talk. No, he can't help that. Anyway, my friend Linda Breslin said that he liked me. She said he was always looking at me during homeroom. She said I should—uh—you know—she was going to Sophomore Night and so was my friend Tina, and naturally . . ."

"I never go to those things. They're dumb."

". . . Karen was going."

"Ahh! She like dances, doesn't she?"

"Let me talk, will you? I'm talking about me now, not Karen."

"Sure, sure! Go ahead, Judy."

"Well, Linda said—I should ask him."

"What's his name again?"

"Henry Wilner."

"Is he the one who's always wiping his nose, has a cold or something?"

"He's allergic to cats."

"Oh him! He's a real turkey."

"That's him. Anyway, she kept telling me to go and ask him. She said we'd have a good time at the dance, and afterward, we'd all go to Farrell's."

"Karen too?"

"Damn it, yes, Karen too. Will you listen to me!"

"I'm listening. I'm listening."

"Anyway, I asked him. Just when the bell rang and my friends were waiting for me out in the hall. I said, 'Hey, Henry, I want to ask you

something.' I tried to be friendly and sort of cute—not the way I am, not the way I want to be. I'll never do that again for anybody. Never! You know, even then, I thought he was some jerk—and I hated myself for doing it."

"So?"

"So I asked him. I said, 'Listen, Henry, I'm thinking of going to Sophomore Night, and I wondered if you—if you would like to go with me.' "

"So what did he say?"

"He said no."

"No what?"

"Just no."

"Just no?"

"Just no, and then he hurried away, and every time he sees me now he turns and goes the other way. Like he's afraid maybe I'll ask him again. And it's not like he's got a girl friend. No girl in the school would even look at him twice. But I had to go and ask him. They were waiting for me in the hall, and I had to go and tell them that Henry Wilner, the school nerd, said no."

"Did you ever think—maybe he's gay? Maybe that's why he said no."

"He's not gay. He doesn't have enough intelligence to be gay."

"You don't have to be intelligent to be gay. Why are you laughing?"

"Because it's so silly. I guess half the bus is hearing what I'm saying. But when it happened, I couldn't tell anybody. Not even my friends. I just said he was going away for that weekend with his parents. They knew I was lying, but nobody said anything. I think they were even more embarrassed than I was."

"Something like that happened to me last year."

"No kidding?"

"Really. Before I moved here, I went to Galileo High, and there was a girl in my homeroom—a nice girl—not pretty, kind of fat, but nice. She laughed a lot, and she liked the movies, and she was always talking about Robert Redford. I figured she'd be easy, so I passed her a note one day. It said that Robert Redford wanted to go to the movies with her, but that he was called out of town suddenly. But I'd be willing to fill in until he came back. And was she free on Saturday night."

"That's cute."

"I thought so too."

"What did she say?"

"She said no."

"Just no?"

"No. Not as bad as with you. She was a nice girl. She said she was tied up that night. Something about an aunt and uncle celebrating their twenty-fifth wedding anniversary, and she had to go."

"Maybe she did."

"I thought if she was really busy, she would have said something like 'I can't go Saturday, but I could Sunday.' Or 'Maybe we could go another night.' I think if she was interested, she would have."

"Not necessarily. You should have asked her."

"I felt funny about it. She should have said something."

"Some girls are too shy."

"Well, some boys are shy too. It's hard being a boy. Everybody expects you to be the one who asks. Then if you get slapped down all the time, it's murder."

"It's worse being a girl. You have to sit around and wait for some boy to ask you. And then, if you like a boy, you can't say anything to him. You have to play this waiting game, and if you're like me, nobody notices you. It's hard."

"Hey, Judy, I think we can help each other."

"I sure hope so."

· 8 ·

WEDNESDAY

"I have an idea."

"What? You'll have to bend over a little more. I can't hear you."

Judy leaned forward in her seat and turned her head up, careful not to let her hair fall back. Today she had pimples down both sides of her face and over her forehead as well. She had combed her hair so that a minimum of face showed through. But she felt happy. Ernie's face looked flushed and eager.

"This is what I'm thinking. You and I both have trouble with the opposite sex, right?"

"Right."

"Okay. So if we eliminate the first step and get on to the second, maybe we'd do better."

"What do you mean?"

"If I invite a boy for you, and you invite Karen for me, then the four of us can go someplace together. It will give the two of us—you and me, I mean—a head start."

"Like what?"

"Like a friend and I have four tickets between us for next Thursday night's ball game at Candlestick Park. You know how the Giants give two free tickets to any student who gets over a 3.5 average."

"You have a 3.5 average?"

"Only for the last marking period. It won't last."

"Don't apologize."

"I'm not apologizing. I wish I was a good student, but I'm not."

"What's your grade point average?"

"About 3.0. What's yours?"

"About 2.8. If it wasn't for biology, I might have had a 3.5 too this marking period. Shaw failed me, and my father carried on so, you would have thought I was a criminal."

"Your father's strict?"

"No, just crazy."

"Mine's dead."

"It's worse having a crazy father."

"No, it's not. It's worse having a dead one."

"Mine fights all the time, especially with me. I'm the oldest."

"What have you got—sisters or brothers?"

"Brothers—two little ones. Joey is eleven, and Larry is eight. They're brats, but my father usually ignores them."

"What about your mother?"

"She's okay. But she works and she's so tired when she gets home, I end up doing a lot of the housework. But she's not bad. It's my father. He's at me all the time."

"My mother works too. She's a nurse. Then I have a sister who's seventeen, and another one who's twelve. The seventeen-year-old one really bugs me. She's bossy and thinks she knows it all."

"What's your mother like?"

"I don't know. She's not home much."

"I wish my father wasn't home much. He has a mail-order business down in the basement. He sells radio-flashlights."

"What?"

"Radio-flashlights. One end's a radio and the other end's a flashlight."

"Sounds neat."

"It isn't. It's dumb. Usually, if the radio is working, the flashlight isn't, and vice versa.

People keep writing angry letters, and somebody or other is always suing him."

"So why doesn't he do something else?"

"Because he's lazy. He can sleep late in the morning, and take a long lunch hour, and be home to pick on me when I get back from school."

"Why does he pick on you?"

"Because he says I'm lazy. Some joke—him telling me that I'm lazy! He says I don't help him enough with his work, and I don't do enough around the house. He's crazy and lazy. Hey, that rhymes. I never realized that before. Listen, I'll make up a poem about him."

I've got a father
Who's lazy.

"Crazy . . . crazy . . . crazy . . . What can I do with 'crazy'?"

"Here, how's this?"

Judy's got a father
She thinks is very lazy.
It's also quite a bother
Because he's rather crazy.

"Hey, that's good. How fast you did that!"

"Oh, that's nothing. I once wrote a poem about my sister that wasn't bad. I guess it's easier to write about people you don't like than about people you do."

"That's crazy, Ernie. Most famous poems are about love."

"Mmm. Anyway, talking about crazy, why are you wearing your hair in that crazy way? Why don't you push it back off your face? You look like a chimpanzee today."

"Look, will you forget about my hair? And I can do without the compliments too. Tell me the poem you wrote about your sister."

"You really want to hear it?"

"Sure I do."

"Okay, here it is."

> There was a young lady named Carrie
> Who knew how to harass and harry.
> She enjoyed day or night
> With her brother to fight
> Who longs for the day she will marry.

"That's funny."

"I used to make them up all the time."

"Do one on me."

"I can't just make one up like that."

"Go ahead—try!"

"Mmm."

"Go ahead. I'll look out the window. It's hard to think when somebody is watching you."

DOGGIE
DINER

She twisted around in her seat. They were passing the Doggie Diner now, which meant that in two more stops they would have to get off. She used to think the bus ride took forever, but lately it went by almost too fast.

"Okay, I've got it."

"That was pretty quick."

> There was a young lady named Judy
> Who was really kind of a cutie.
> When I said that her hair
> Was making me stare
> She gave me a look rather snooty.

"That stinks."

"I did it in less than a minute. You have to remember that."

"Okay, but we'd better move. Here's our stop now."

· 9 ·

THURSDAY

"I never finished telling you my plan yesterday."

"First let me tell you something."

"What?"

"I started writing a poem about you."

"No kidding!"

"Do you want to hear it?"

"Sure."

> I know a boy whose name is Russe.
> His nose is long, his mouth is loose.

"Well?"

"That's all so far. I'm not finished."

"You know something? Nobody ever wrote a

poem about me before. Thanks a lot—it's just great."

"That's all right. Anyway, what's your plan?"

"Oh—that's right. Well, we have these tickets for next Thursday night. What I was thinking was—maybe you could ask Karen to go for me. And I'll ask Alex to take you."

"Who?"

"Alex. Alex Zimmer."

"Who's Alex Zimmer?"

"He's a friend of mine and he has the other two tickets. You'll like him."

"How do you know I'll like him?"

"Well, let's try, okay? It's not as if you have somebody else in mind, right?"

"How do you know I don't have anybody else in mind?"

"Well, who then?"

"How about Tom Kerny?"

"Tom Kerny? Are you crazy?"

"No, why am I crazy?"

"He's the best-looking boy in school—and the most popular."

"Well, Karen is the best-looking girl in school, and just as popular."

"It's not the same thing."

"Why not? If I get a date for you with the

best-looking girl in school, then you should do the same for me."

"Do you know Tom Kerny?"

"No."

"Well, neither do I. So it's not the same thing. Both of us know Karen. She's your friend."

"She's sort of my friend."

"I can't just go up to Tom Kerny and ask him to go to a baseball game."

"Why not?"

"I just told you—I don't know him. Anyway, Alex has the tickets."

"What does he look like?"

"He's thin and very muscular. He was captain of the soccer team, and he's about five feet ten—a little taller than me."

"Is he good-looking?"

"I guess he's okay. He's kind of shy."

"Does he have bushy brown hair and sort of a big mouth?"

"I guess his hair is kind of bushy."

"And he's pigeon-toed?"

"Well—maybe a little bit. Lots of athletes are."

"I think he's in my creative writing class. He never opens his mouth."

"I told you he was shy. But a girl like you, who's so talky . . ."

"I'm not talky. I'm shy."

"That'll be the day. Anyway, you'll like him when you get to know him."

"Judging by how much he talks, that should be in about forty years."

"Come on, Judy, don't be such a smart ass."

"I'm not a smart ass, but I don't have a very positive impression of him. Did you say anything about me?"

"Not yet. I wanted to check with you first."

"I'd rather go with Tom Kerny."

"Don't start that again. Look, I have an idea. Why don't I come by your typing class today with Alex, and maybe you and Karen . . ."

"I have a speech-team meeting."

"Well, how about tomorrow, Judy? Alex and I could meet you, and the four of us could have lunch. Maybe I could just say we have these four tickets. I could sort of mention it to you, and you could say something like 'Great! I'd like to come.' Then maybe you could say to Karen, 'Why don't we all go? We'd have a blast!' "

"I don't say things like that."

"Like what?"

"Like 'We'd have a blast!' That's not my style."

"Say it any way you like, but say it."

"Suppose I don't like him."

"You will. Everybody likes him when they get to know him."

"We'll have to arrange a signal."

"What?"

"If I don't like him, I'll do something. And then you won't say anything about the tickets."

"Like what?"

"Like I'll say, 'Boy, this is one lousy sandwich!' That means 'Forget it.' Nobody will be suspicious. Okay?"

"Okay, but I hope I remember."

"You better."

"So, it's all set then. Alex and I will come by tomorrow after fourth period, and you'll talk to Karen before. Does she usually bring lunch?"

"Yes."

"Well, we can go over near the football field, or wherever she likes."

"I like to eat lunch near the girls' gym."

"Why don't we decide tomorrow. Okay?"

"Ernie, you're forgetting something."

"What?"

"She already has a boyfriend."

"I'm just inviting her to go to a baseball game. No big deal about that."

"Maybe she'll be seeing her boyfriend that night."

"Maybe, maybe not. I figure she sees him on the weekends, so she'll probably be free Thursday nights."

"She's really crazy about him."

"How do you know?"

"She told me."

"Mmm."

"I think she generally sees him Thursdays. Yes, I think she said that."

"Well, let's just go ahead and try. Okay?"

"Mmm."

· 10 ·

MONDAY

"Well, what happened to you Friday?"

"I had a sore throat."

"I thought maybe you missed the bus or caught an earlier one. You could have called me."

"I didn't have your number."

"There's only one Russe in the phone book."

"Well, by the time I decided I was too sick to go to school, it would have been too late to call you anyway. I couldn't help getting sick, you know. You don't have to sound so mad."

"I know. I know. But it nearly screwed up my plans."

"Tough!"

"Anyway, she was real sweet."

"Who was?"

"Karen."

"Oh, did you talk to her Friday?"

"Yes, I did. Alex and I were waiting outside the room after the period ended. She came out and smiled. She looked so cute. She had on a blue T-shirt that said Hands Off on the front, and had two hands over her . . ."

"I know that T-shirt. Did you talk to her?"

"She talked to me. She actually came over and talked to me."

"She didn't . . . I mean . . . you didn't say anything about her boyfriend?"

"No, of course not. I told her Alex and I were friends of yours. . . ."

"Why'd you say that? Alex isn't a friend of mine. I don't know him. I don't even think I like him."

"Calm down! Wait till you hear how everything worked out."

"Worked out?"

"Uh-huh. I told her we were supposed to meet you for lunch. She said you were absent. I said, 'Too bad.' She said yes, it was too bad. I said maybe we'd try again Monday. She said maybe we should. Then I—you're going to be surprised—then I said, real cool, maybe she'd like to come too. And you know what?"

"What?"

HANDS
OFF!

"She said, 'Great!' No kidding. She said 'Great!' like she really meant it. And, listen to this, she said she'd bake some cookies. She said she'd call you."

"She didn't."

"Maybe she didn't know your number."

"There's only one Koppelmacker in the phone book."

"Well, she sounded happy, like she really was looking forward to it. She said she loves to eat lunch out of doors, and especially over near the football field."

"I like it better near the girls' gym."

"We'll decide later."

"I don't know if I can come."

"Why not?"

"I think I'm supposed to see my counselor."

"During lunch?"

"I think she said during lunch."

"Well, if you can't come, we'll just have to go ahead without you."

"I'll try to come."

"Who's your counselor, anyway?"

"Mrs. Jenkins."

"She's mine too. What do you think of her?"

"She doesn't listen."

"She does to me."

"Maybe she likes you. I don't think she likes me. Somebody said she doesn't like girls."

"When I was having all that trouble with Shaw, I went to see her, and she was real nice."

"I went to see her about Shaw too, and she wasn't even sympathetic. I told her I couldn't afford an F because I wanted to go to U.C. Berkeley—and you know what she said?"

"What?"

"She said I couldn't get into Berkeley anyway. That my grade point average wasn't good enough, and that my PSAT scores were lousy. Who needs a counselor to tell you that? I told her I knew a couple of kids who got in with lower GPA's, and she said I was wrong."

"Maybe you were."

"No, I wasn't, but she didn't listen to me. She said she had to see some other people. I hate her."

"So why do you want to go see her again?"

"I don't."

"But you said before that you had to see her during lunch today."

"Well, maybe I won't go."

"Judy, you want to go to U.C. Berkeley?"

"Uh-huh."

"What are you interested in?"

"I want to be a doctor."

"And you're failing biology?"

"That's not my fault. Anyway, what about you? What do you want to do?"

"I don't know."

"Well, isn't there something you're interested in?"

"No."

"Nothing?"

"Not to work at all my life."

"What are you good at?"

"Nothing."

"Oh, come off it, Russe. You must be good at something."

"No, I'm not. Lots of things I like to do, but I'm just not good at anything."

"How can you say that? Everybody's good at something."

"I'm not."

"That's terrible."

"I think so too."

"But you're smiling."

"Because I feel terrible. I always smile when I feel terrible. Otherwise I'd probably cry. Like this fall—Alex got me to join the soccer team. I like soccer, and he said I'd probably be good at it. But I spent most of the season on the bench. One time I got to play because three guys were out

with the flu. I managed to trip one of our own men while he was carrying the ball."

"Soccer's not everything."

"No—but I tried out for the baseball team last spring. I really love baseball. I'm like a computer. Just give me a player—any player who ever lived—go ahead—I'll probably be able to tell you his batting average. Go on!"

"I don't know anything about baseball."

"Go on. Any player."

"Uh . . . Babe Ruth."

"Okay—forget it! Anyway, they put me on the junior varsity team. Even there I spent most of the season on the bench."

"Sports aren't everything."

"I know. That's what I tell myself, but it's other things too. I'm not really good at anything. And I want to be. I want to be good at something—at anything—but I don't know what. And sometimes I'm scared."

"Of what?"

"That it'll always be like that. That I'll go through life always sitting on the bench, waiting."

He wasn't smiling now. He wasn't looking at her either. He was looking over her head, and his eyes were tight and narrowed. It made her nervous, seeing him all folded up into himself like that. Something began hurting down low in her stomach.

She put out an arm and murmured, "Ernie . . . don't, Ernie. Come on, Ernie, it's going to be all right."

He took a deep breath, and then he was smiling again. He looked into her face, and he said, "You know something, Judy? Your hair looks even crazier today than usual."

· 11 ·

TUESDAY

"So?"

"So what?"

"What did you think?"

"It's nice of you to be interested in what I think."

"We really had a good time, didn't we?—The four of us, I mean. Alex liked you. He said you were really interesting."

"I don't know how he could tell that, considering I didn't open my mouth once. You and Karen were doing all the talking."

"She's really easy to talk to, isn't she? I mean, you wouldn't think such a beautiful girl would be so sweet, would you?"

"Mmm."

"I mean, she was really interested in what I had to say."

"Especially since everything you had to say was about her."

"Not everything. We talked about all sorts of things—and she really knows a lot about baseball. Hey, wasn't it great what happened when I said we had four tickets? Right off, she said, 'Oh, I'd love to go. Could I buy a ticket from you?' Didn't that work out just great?"

"Say, you know, I'm kind of p.o.'d at you. Didn't we agree that you weren't going to say anything about the tickets if I said 'Boy, this is one lousy sandwich'? And I said it two times."

"I guess I forgot. I'm sorry, Judy. But Alex is a nice guy, isn't he? You both seemed to be getting along okay."

"He's weird."

"How can you say he's weird?"

"Easy. I'll say it again. He's weird."

"Come on, Judy. You'll have a good time Thursday night. You'll see. Alex drives, and his father will let him have the car. And we were thinking we'd treat you and Karen to dinner at Candlestick Park."

"No thanks."

"Why not?"

"First of all, I don't eat that garbage they sell at

Candlestick Park. You know what's inside those hot dogs?"

"No, but you can have a sandwich if you don't like the hot dogs."

"And besides, I like to pay my own way when I go out with boys. What's funny about that?"

"Oh, nothing."

"Come on, what's so funny?"

"It's just that you said— Come on, Judy, you've never been out with a boy before, so how can you say 'when I go out with boys'?"

"Look, you're stepping on my feet."

"Oh, I'm sorry."

She wanted to step on *his* feet. Maybe even kick him a good one in the shins. She wanted to say something mean and cruel, and most of all, she wanted to get away from him. But they were packed in too tight, as usual. Too tight even to squeeze her way through to the back.

"Well, you haven't ever been out with a girl either."

"I never said I had. But never mind, if you want to pay your own way, you can."

"I do."

"I wonder what Karen thinks."

"Oh, she doesn't mind boys paying for her. She's used to it. Her boyfriend spends a fortune

on her every time they go out. Last time he took her to Trader Vic's."

"Trader Vic's! I don't know—Maybe she'd be insulted if I bought her a hot dog at Candlestick Park. What do you think I should do, Judy?"

"I think—well—I think we should each pay our own way."

"Okay, I'll do whatever you say. Are you a women's libber, Judy?"

"Sure, I'm for it."

"I guess I am too. Except that I think I'm really for everybody's lib—men's as well as women's."

"Men are already liberated."

"Says who?"

"Everybody knows that. They get the best jobs and the highest salaries, and people respect men more than women."

"That's bull. Nobody respects me in my house, and I have two sisters and one mother, so I'm the only male."

"My father doesn't think girls need to go to college. He says he's not going to pay for medical school for me, but if one of my brothers wants to go, that's different."

"The way you're doing in biology, he won't have to worry. But no kidding, Judy, it's no picnic being a male either. Sometimes my mother and sisters go off into my mother's bedroom and talk

and giggle. Sometimes they all sleep there—the three of them in my mother's bed. I can hear them talking and laughing."

"Ernie, you're jealous."

"I'm excluded just because I'm a boy. It's not fair."

"I wish my father would exclude me. You ought to come over to my house sometime, Ernie. You'd be glad you're not a girl."

"I don't want to be a girl. I just want to be me. I want to be able to talk to people and not think I can't because I'm a boy."

"What do you mean?"

"Come over here, near the door. I don't want anybody to hear."

"Is this okay?"

"I guess so. I'm talking low. Can you hear me?"

"Sure I can, Ernie."

"See, my mother goes out with a doctor in the hospital. She's been going with him for a year or so."

"What kind of a doctor?"

"An orthopedist."

"Where did he go to school?"

"How should I know. Judy, will you listen to me?"

"You're raising your voice."

"Oh, never mind."

"Go ahead, Ernie. I'm sorry. I'm listening."

"Well, sometimes she brings him home and I hear them late at night in her bedroom."

"In her bedroom!"

"Shh! Let me finish, Judy. I never told anybody this before. Sometimes my sisters hear them, and lots of times they fight."

"Who fights?"

"My older sister, Carrie. She yells at my mother and my mother yells back. Sometimes, after it's over, I hear my mother crying. I want to go and talk to her. I want to tell her I don't feel the way Carrie does—that I'm not mad at her because she's involved with the doctor. I want to tell her not to cry and that I love her and want her to be happy."

"So why don't you?"

"Because I'm a boy, and I don't know if she'd like me to. When you're little, it doesn't matter whether you're a girl or a boy. When my father died I was only seven. I used to hear her at night, crying. I'd go into her room and climb in bed with her, and put my arms around her and say, 'I love you, Mom. Don't cry anymore.' Then she'd kiss me, and after a while she'd laugh and say I was her favorite boy. It was sort of a joke, see, because I'm the only boy."

"Yes, I see."

"But now I hardly talk to her anymore. I want to but there I am, inside myself, inside being a boy, and she's out there—and I can't talk to her. Sometimes I think maybe she wants me to, and I don't know what to do."

"So go ahead and talk to her."

"But I can't."

"Sure you can. You're talking to me, aren't you? And you don't even know me the way you know her."

"It's easier talking to a stranger."

"We're not strangers, Ernie."

"No, I guess we're not anymore."

"Talk to her, Ernie. You'll see. You'll feel better and so will she."

"I don't know, but anyway, Judy, thanks."

"For what?"

"For listening."

· 12 ·

WEDNESDAY

"I was thinking about you."

"Good or bad?"

"Good, naturally. You're a nice kid, and now I'm going to do you a real favor."

"And what's that?"

"I'm going to give you some advice."

"The answer is no."

"But how do you know you won't like it if you won't even try?"

"I know."

"But Judy, you look so funny with your hair that way. All you have to do is just comb it back. Why are you hiding your face?"

"Okay, I'll show you why. Here, hold my books. Now, look!"

"Oh!"

"All right? Now, stop bothering me!"

"Why didn't you say so?"

"Just come right out, you mean, to somebody I hardly know, and say, 'The reason I wear my hair over my face is because I have pimples.' Oh, that's just great!"

"But I still think . . ."

"Shut up, Russe!"

"Okay, okay, let's change the subject."

"Good idea. Uh . . . what are you wearing tomorrow night to the game?"

"I don't know. How about you?"

"I don't know."

"Better dress warm. It can get pretty cold at Candlestick Park."

"Well, maybe I'll wear my jeans and a sweater."

"That yellow one."

"You mean my old yellow sweater with the red buttons?"

"I like that sweater."

"My father hates it. He says I look like the face of Death in it."

"I like it. It's a nice color, and it looks good next to your dark hair."

"I have a pink sweater that my mother gave me for Christmas."

"I hate pink."

"And a blue one with white stars embroidered on it."

"Maybe I'll come by this afternoon and check out your wardrobe. I mean, unless you're going to be busy or something."

"No, I'm not going to be busy, but that sounds weird—having you come over to look at my sweaters."

"I could say something but I won't. Since you're not going to let me advise you on your hairstyle, I may as well act as your fashion consultant. Besides, I like those cookies your mother bakes."

"My mother doesn't bake cookies."

"Well, my sister does—chocolate oatmeal cookies. I'll bring some of those. Where do you live?"

"516 Lawrence."

"What time do you get home?"

"About three-thirty."

"I'll come by about four. Okay?"

"Okay, but don't bring any cookies."

"Why not?"

"It's not good for my skin."

"You don't have to eat any."

"But I will if you bring them, and I'm not

supposed to eat chocolate. We always have graham crackers at home. We could eat those."

"The sacrifices one makes in the name of friendship."

· 13 ·

THURSDAY

"How come you're not wearing it?"

"I'll put it on later before we go. But I thought you didn't like pink."

"I usually don't, but that pink is such a pretty color, and the sweater is so soft and fuzzy."

"I never wore it before."

"I bet Alex will like it."

"Oh yeah—Alex! I forgot about Alex."

"Your father doesn't seem like such a bad guy. He was very friendly. It was interesting seeing that setup he has down in the basement."

"He liked you too. He said you were very intelligent."

"Naturally."

"But that's only because you let him do all the

talking, and you acted interested in everything he said. He's such a windbag. He can go on and on for hours."

"I really was interested in what he was saying."

"Oh yeah? What was he saying?"

"Oh—lots of things."

"Go on—name one."

"Well, let's see. He said somebody else had the idea for a radio-flashlight at the same time he did, but the other man died before he could get his business started. And he also said that you were so quick and handy, he didn't need to hire anybody else."

"He said that?"

"Sure he did."

"I didn't hear him."

"Maybe you were on the phone then."

"Maybe. Why doesn't he ever say anything nice to me?"

"He also said you took after him. He hopes you and he could be partners after you finish school."

"I'm going to be a doctor. I don't want to be his partner."

"He said you were smarter than your brothers, and had a real business head."

"He said that?"

"Uh-huh."

"I don't believe it."

"He really did."

"The hypocrite! He says one thing to my face and another behind my back. All he wants from me is work, work, work. And he's never satisfied. He doesn't ever bug my brothers, but with me—he's never off my back for one second."

"Maybe it's because he thinks a lot of you."

"I don't think so."

"I do."

"I don't."

"Well, now that we're finished with that subject, let's go on to another. I want to ask you if you like this shirt I'm wearing."

"No."

"Why not?"

"It's ugly."

"Why is it ugly? I just bought it a few days ago at Jeff's Jeans."

"It's like what all the hoods are wearing."

"I don't know any hoods with a shirt like this."

"Besides, I don't like black shirts. Why don't you wear your green Mickey Mouse one?"

"That old, crummy shirt! I've had that since junior high. The sleeves are too short."

"I like it."

"Nobody wears shirts like that anymore."

"I like it."

"Well, I think I'm going to wear this shirt. I

bought it especially for tonight. And I can wear my red sweater over it."

"Yuk!"

"You really don't like it?"

"I told you already."

"Well, what about Karen? Do you think she'll like it?"

"No, I don't. Her boyfriend is a real classy dresser."

"How do you know?"

"She told me. He wears Pierre Cardin suits, and buys all his shirts at Brooks Brothers."

"That's crazy! I thought you said he went to City College because he didn't have any money to go anywhere else."

"I never said that."

"I could have sworn you did."

"No, I think he goes to City because his mother is sick and she needs him. He's a very kind, good person."

"Oh!"

"He has beautiful manners and exquisite taste."

"You really think I should wear the Mickey Mouse shirt?"

"I really do."

"You think it's in better taste? What's so funny?"

She couldn't help laughing. His face looked so mournful. He was watching her laugh, and then suddenly he was laughing too. There were crinkly laugh lines all around his small, bright eyes, and his whole face shone."

"Ouch! Why'd you step on my feet?"

"Because you're making fun of me. Ouch! Cut it out!"

"There! You deserve it. Hey, be careful—I'm dropping my books."

"Watch it— Ha! There—you hit that lady. Oh boy!"

"I'm sorry. I really am."

"It's really my fault, miss. I pushed her. . . . All right . . . we'll calm down. I'm sorry."

"Here, Ernie, over here. There's a little room."

"Stop laughing! She's looking."

"Everybody's looking."

"Well, you stop first."

"I can't."

Every time the bus jiggled them against each other or against somebody else, they laughed so hard they couldn't keep their balance. There were angry faces all around them.

"Okay, now we really have to stop. Ernie, stop it!"

"I can't. . . . I can't. . . . I can't."

· 14 ·

FRIDAY

"So?"

"So what?"

"What'd you think?"

"He's a nerd."

"Vida Blue?"

"No, not Vida Blue. Your friend, the big talker, Alex Zimmer."

"Did you ever hear 'Still waters run deep'?"

"I heard it but now I don't believe it. Now I just think Still waters run stupid."

"You looked cute last night."

"Thanks a lot."

"And wasn't it funny how Karen was wearing pink too?"

"Very funny."

"She has such a good sense of humor. I don't know where she gets those crazy shirts of hers—they're really far-out."

"There's a T-shirt store on Sutter where you can buy them. Lots of kids have them."

"I never saw one that said Push on the back, and Pull on the front."

"I have."

"I haven't."

"I have."

"Well, there's another topic of conversation settled unanimously. Let's talk about something else. Did Karen say anything about me?"

"When?"

"Last night."

"You were there all the time, weren't you?"

"I mean when the two of you went off to the ladies' room."

"No."

"She didn't say anything?"

"No."

"No what?"

"Just no."

"I mean, do you mean 'No, she didn't say anything' or 'No, she did say something'?"

"I mean no."

"She likes you a lot."

"When did she say anything about me? The

two of you didn't go off to the ladies' room, did you?"

"Very funny. No, when I walked her upstairs. After we dropped you off, I mean. She said you're a great person."

"Mmm."

"And you know something, Judy?"

"What?"

"She looked so sweet and friendly, and she kept saying what a great time she had. I said—no kidding, I really did—I said, 'Well, let's do it again.' "

"Mmm."

"And you know what she said?"

"What?"

"She said 'When?' "

"Just like that?"

"Just like that. She's so easy to talk to. I never thought she'd be that friendly."

"Mmm."

"So I said, 'When are you free?' And you won't believe what she said."

"What was that?"

"She said, 'Saturday night.' "

"I'm not surprised."

"But what about her boyfriend? I thought she'd be going out with him. I figured maybe she'd say

21
PULL

Tuesday or Wednesday—one of those nothing nights."

"You didn't mention her boyfriend, did you?"

"Of course not, Judy."

"Because I told you lots of things in confidence."

"I know that, Judy."

"I wouldn't want her to think . . ."

"I'm not going to say anything about her boyfriend—but Judy, what do you think? Do you think she likes me?"

"Yes, I think she likes you."

"I can't believe it."

"Why shouldn't she like you, Ernie? You're the kind of person . . . Lots of people would like a person like you."

"No, they don't, Judy. I know you don't think so, but I'm really very shy. You're the first person besides Alex I've ever really talked to."

"He must be a fantastic listener. Last night, I don't think he said three words all evening."

"He's pretty quiet, I guess. But he thought you were quiet too. He said he thought you were shy."

"See."

"I told him you weren't. I said you always had plenty to say to me, but he . . ."

"What?"

"Well, he . . . thought you were shy."

"He didn't like me, did he?"

"It's not that he didn't like you exactly. . . ."

"It's not that he did like me exactly either, right? Well, that's okay because I don't like him either, so we're even."

"Okay, but I haven't forgotten my promise to you."

"Forget it."

"No, you really helped me to get to know Karen, and now it's my turn to help you. Who would you like to go out with?"

"I already told you—Tom Kerny."

"I don't know Tom Kerny. How about somebody else?"

"Well, what about Jay Lindeman?"

"He's a jock."

"I know he's a jock—he's quarterback on the football team, isn't he?"

"He's an idiot. Not for you. Who else?"

"There isn't anybody else I like except—well—Do you know Jeff Choy?"

"Sure I know him. He's in my American history class."

"Well, I'll tell you something. He's the captain of the speech team. I know all about him, but he doesn't really know me—just to say hello. He came to my English class last term and tried to get us to join the speech team. And I did because he seemed so . . ."

"You like Jeff Choy?"

"He's such a nice boy and a smart one too."

"I don't think he's so smart."

"He keeps winning all sorts of prizes in the tournaments. He's great at debate. I kept thinking maybe I should ask him to give me a few pointers. I never have but I keep thinking I should."

"He's sort of stuck-up. Likes to think he's smarter than everybody else."

"No, he's not like that at all. Everybody likes him."

"I don't."

"Well, that's your hard luck."

"Listen, Judy, he's too square for you. He goes to all those dumb dances and he dresses like a real dude."

"You know—I guess I should be honest with you, Ernie."

"I thought you were, Judy. I've been honest with you."

"Well, so have I—up to a point. But I never told you about Jeff because— You know the way you feel about Karen? I should have understood

it and been more sympathetic. It's the way you feel about a dream—something beautiful and far off. Something that maybe won't ever come true but it's there for you to have—only for you whether it comes true or not."

"I know."

"Well, now maybe you and Karen will work something out, but I've liked Jeff for a long time—maybe a few years. I knew him in junior high, and I always thought he was the nicest person I ever knew."

"Jeff Choy?"

"And I never told anybody about him. Not even my girl friends. Because it was really something that only belonged to me. You know there were other boys I liked. Isn't it funny how you can like several people at the same time?"

"I know what you mean."

"But one is the deep, most important one—like Jeff. And the others—Tom Kerny and Jay Lindeman—they come and go. They're replaceable, but not the deep one."

"You feel that way about Jeff?"

"I used to."

"You still do?"

"No, I guess not anymore. I guess I don't. Maybe that's why I was able to tell you about him. Because I don't. I guess there's nobody right now I'm interested in."

"Well, that's okay then, Judy. Let's both think it over. You look around and let me see what I can come up with. We'll work something out. You've done a lot for me, Judy, and I'm not going to forget it."

"I didn't do anything for you, Ernie. You did it yourself."

· 15 ·

MONDAY

"Had a nice weekend?"

"No, but I guess you did."

"Why do you say that?"

"Because you're grinning from ear to ear."

"So tell me what you did this weekend."

"Me? Nothing special. You're the one who had the great time. Right?"

"Right."

"So what did you do?"

"No, you tell me first."

"You're really a slob, Ernie Russe, you know that? But okay, I'll tell you what I did. Saturday morning, I sat down at the breakfast table, and my mother said, 'Eat something.' I said, 'I'm not hungry.' She said, 'Breakfast is the most impor-

tant meal of the day. Have an egg.' I told her, 'No, I don't want an egg.' You want me to go on?"

"Uh-huh. I want to know everything you did."

"Same conversation at lunch. In between, I dusted and vacuumed, and my father complained that I did a lousy job. Saturday afternoon, I took my brothers shopping for some socks and underwear at Sears. Later my aunt came over and told us all the latest details about her high blood pressure. That about wraps up Saturday."

"What did you do at night?"

"What I always do Saturday night. I watched TV and ate a salami sandwich and went to bed."

"Mustard or mayonnaise?"

"What?"

"On the sandwich."

"Okay, Russe, I don't know what kind of game you're playing, but I quit. You're not funny, and if you don't want to talk about your big date, it's okay with me."

"No, I do, Koppelmacker. I want to talk about it. I do. I just wanted to make a little comparison."

"Between how I spent Saturday and how you spent it? Thanks a lot."

"I want to ask you something, Judy. What do you think of Karen?"

"Honestly?"

"Of course, honestly."

"She's . . . she's a nice girl."

"I think so too."

"I know you think so."

"But I wanted to know what you thought."

"She's a nice girl. She was always a nice girl. I never told you this but we used to be very close friends in fifth grade. She was little and chubby then, but everybody liked her just like now."

"I wasn't sure you liked her."

"I do. I don't want to but I do."

"What do you mean?"

"Well, we're not close friends anymore like we used to be. She was really my first best friend. I wasn't anything special, just like now, but she picked me for her friend."

"Why?"

"I don't know. Somebody said it was because I made her look good, but it wasn't so. We had fun together. All sorts of special, private games. We had a secret club—just for her and me—and we had secret names. Mine was Nerak and hers was Yduj. That's Karen and Judy spelled backwards."

"So what do you mean you don't want to like her?"

"Well, because she's so—successful. She can't help herself. She makes people feel good. Even teachers always liked her best. You could see they tried to act like they liked all the kids in the class but she was always teacher's pet."

"She can't help herself if people like her."

"That's what I said. She's smart too, and good at lots of things. In sixth grade, our class gave a play. I wanted one of the parts. It was a princess who cried all the time. I tried out for it, and I was lousy. She got the part and she was great. She couldn't help it—being so good, I mean—but I was so jealous I wouldn't talk to her for a few weeks."

"What did she do?"

"She kept trying to make up with me, and finally we did. But then she made more friends, and I got jealous again. She kept asking me to go places with her and her friends, and I felt like I was just tagging along. So after a while, I just stopped going."

"She really likes you."

"I guess she does. She likes everybody."

"What does that mean?"

"I can't—like everybody, I mean. A lot of the time I don't even like myself. It was too heavy—being her friend, I mean."

"We talked about you a lot."

"It must have been a great evening."

"It was. And we talked about somebody else too."

"Who?"

"Guess."

"Why are you grinning?"

"Guess."

"I don't know. Who did you talk about?"

"Guess."

"I said I don't know. What's with you today?"

"Do you give up?"

"Okay, I give up."

"We talked about her boyfriend."

"Oh!"

"He's evidently quite a person."

"Look, Ernie . . ."

"No, he's everything you said and more—good-looking, smart, rich, marvelous taste—all those Pierre Cardin suits and Brooks Brothers shirts. And what about his Jaguar? You forgot to mention his Jaguar."

"You're mad, aren't you, Ernie?"

"At first I was. I figured it was maybe because you hated her or something."

"No, I just told you, I like her. I don't want to but I do. If I hate anybody, it's myself. I guess you'll hate me too after this."

"I couldn't figure it out at first—why you lied to me about him. I thought you were my friend, and here you handed me all this bull about an imaginary boyfriend. I said to Karen . . ."

"You told Karen?"

"Not that you told me she had a boyfriend. We were talking about friends, and she said she knew some kids at City. I asked her who. She started naming a whole bunch of people but not Alan. So I asked her if she knew somebody named Alan who went to City College. She said no. I thought maybe she didn't want to say anything, but I told her somebody I knew said she had a boyfriend named Alan who went to City. I didn't say anything about you. She said no. She used to go around with a boy named Rodney who went to State College but she never even knew an Alan anywhere. I believed her too because I don't think she's a liar."

"No, she's not a liar."

"I thought about it all day yesterday. I nearly called you to tell you off, but finally I think I have it all worked out."

"Why don't we forget the whole thing. What difference does it make anyway?"

"Oh, it makes a lot of difference."

"I don't see why. So I'm a nerd. But you got to go out with Karen, and I guess she likes you."

"I guess she does."

"I knew she would. I told you she would. Didn't I?"

"But Karen likes everybody, and I'm not sure I

want to stand around watching her be friendly with the whole world. Especially since I think I may have an alternative."

"Oh?"

"You know you're looking great today, Judy. At least whatever it is I can see of you looks great. That is your nose showing out from under your hair, isn't it?"

"Very funny."

"And you're wearing your pink sweater today. Hey, Judy, how come you're wearing your pink sweater today?"

"Honestly?"

"Of course, honestly."

"Because Karen called me yesterday."

"She called you?"

"Uh-huh."

"Why did she call you?"

"To talk about you."

"What did she say?"

"Oh, she said she liked you. . . ."

"Naturally."

"But . . ."

"Ah . . ."

"But . . . she thought . . . She said you kept talking about . . ."

"Her boyfriend?"

"No, she didn't mention her boyfriend. It's a

good thing she didn't mention her boyfriend or I might have been sick today. But she said you kept talking about me, and she thought . . . well . . ."

"Judy?"

"What?"

"Remember what they told us in sophomore English?"

"What?"

"About a double negative."

"I forget."

"You know how a double negative makes a positive. Two no's make a yes. So what do you think? Do you think two losers can make one winning combination?"

He was smiling at her now. Every part of his face was smiling. It was a funny face, but the nicest one she'd ever seen in her whole life. He moved up closer now, and waited for her to speak.

"Ernie . . ."

"What?"

"Get off my feet."